Secret Keys

Stories that
unlock a child's potential

Illustrated by Peter Ambush and Anthony Woolridge

REVIEW AND HERALD® PUBLISHING ASSOCIATION
HAGERSTOWN, MD 21740

Edited by Carmela A. Monk
Designed by Bill Kirstein
Cover design by Helcio Deslandes
Illustrations by Peter Ambush and Anthony Woolridge

Written by Betty Dennis Brown, Bill Cleveland, Reuben Escalante, Nona Turner Grant, Patricia Humphrey, Charles Mills, Carolyn Stuyvesant, Sergio Torres, Elizabeth Watson, and Bernice Webster

Activities by Celeste perrino Walker

Editorial Staff
Delbert Baker   Stephen Ruff
Bill Cleveland   Carol Thomas

Project Consultants
Faith Crumbly   Jocelyn Johnson   Su Lan Tan
Randy Fishell   Lolethia Morgan   Carol Wallington   Ron Pride
Elsie Hall   Jocelyn Reid   Patricia Wegh   Lee Cherry

MESSAGE Books is a division of the
Review and Herald® Publishing Association,
Hagerstown, Maryland 21740

PRINTED IN U.S.A.

03 02   8 7

R&H Cataloging Service
    Secret keys: stories that unlock your child's potential.

    1. Values—stories. 2 Biography—juvenile works. 3. Spiritual life—stories
                            808.89

ISBN 0-8280-0724-1

Dedication

Secret Keys help us become better people.
They help us respect others.
And they lead to success and happiness.

So we dedicate these SECRET KEYS to:

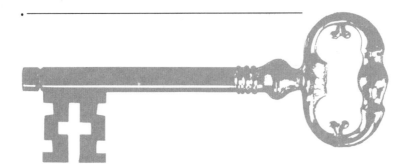

Use them wisely.

Contents

1

Hidden Keys

The Golden Opportunity

I DON'T *know why I can't get this!* Stanley stared hard at his math book. His eyebrows went up and down. He rested his head on one elbow and then the other. Nothing worked. His math test was tomorrow, and he had spent just too much time playing soccer. Now he was trying to cram several months of studying into one night. It wasn't working.

"I'm going to flunk, and those guys are all going to get A's. That's just not fair!" Ed had given Stanley a "golden opportunity." And he'd blown it.

Earlier that afternoon, after school, the soccer guys had met, under the stadium. There, under the bleachers, only the warm Bermudian sun and ocean breeze could find them. They always met in this secret place to discuss the game and other things.

"You guys must promise not to tell anyone what I'm going to say right now," said Ed.

"OK, we promise," the friends agreed.

They often shared secrets. But today Ed dropped a real bombshell. "I know what's going to be on the math test tomorrow!"

"What?" That grabbed their attention. "You're kidding!"

"I kid you not," said Ed. "I bought the answers from that new kid, Sam. You know, the one who just came from the States?"

"Yeah, that guy who's always fiddling around with his computer," Stanley said. "He's not in our class. Why would he have the questions to our test?"

"Well, I'm not sure; he wasn't too clear. He used his modem and some connection through the school's phone lines to get into the computer in the teachers' lounge."

"Well, so what? Our teacher could have taken her disk home."

"He says that the computer stored her math test. He used the telephone to call it up on his screen. I'm telling you, he's got it!"

"So what do we do?"

"He wants $10 and a pledge to forget everything."

"Ten dollars? That's kind of high."

"Yeah, but you know we've been slacking off this whole school year," said Ed. "I won't make it to the next

level without acing this quiz. Count me in."

"Me too," said another.

"What about you, Stanley?"

Stanley's head was spinning. He wanted to go to the next level with his class. These were his friends, the guys he hung out with. But as a Christian he knew he couldn't cheat and follow the example of Jesus too. Maybe he could, though, just this once.

"I, uh . . ." No, his lips just couldn't say the words. What a time to have an attack of honesty.

"Not me, guys; count me out. I'm going to study and try to ace the test." Several other guys also refused. The rest of them raced off to find Sam.

The next day, as Mrs. Ottley quietly passed out the tests, Stanley worried. He had studied, and he had prayed. Stanley still didn't have many answers in his head, though.

"At least I didn't cheat!" Stanley said to himself. He looked around. Most of the guys looked really relaxed.

"Class, you have 35 minutes to finish the test. You may look down now and start," said Mrs. Ottley.

It was worse than Stanley thought. He wasn't doing too well. When he finished, he knew that he would have to repeat math next year. This time without any afternoon soccer games.

Later, when the teacher posted the test scores, Stanley felt bad. He was near the bottom of the class, while all the guys who had bought tests had gotten A's and had passed.

"Dad, that just isn't fair," Stanley said to his father at home that night. "I tried to do what Jesus wanted me to do, and I failed while those guys went on. It just isn't fair!"

"Son, your mother and I are very proud of you—for not cheating, that is. We saw how hard you studied these last three days. You know, though, that you should have been doing that all along. Your real problem is soccer, not your schoolwork. And some of your choices for friends haven't been good either. Do you want to tell the headmaster about the cheating?"

"I can't, Dad. I made a promise to the guys.

"Even so, you may have to speak up eventually. I've heard that the headmaster suspects some tampering with the school computer. If his suspicions are true, he'll expel the students who cheated. That's a lot worse than failing. The cheaters may not get away with this. But even if they do, they'll probably be looking over their shoulders for the next few months."

Stanley's dad smiled. "Remember one point, son. You're learning things that will help you when you grow up. Your honesty is more important than a passing grade. Soon those guys who sold their honor for an A will find that they are the real losers!"

BY BILL CLEVELAND

KEY BOX

SECRET KEY:
Practice honesty in everything. Your honor is worth more than temporary gain.

THINK ABOUT IT:
Would it be worth it to you to lie if you were in Stanley's position?

GO FOR IT:
Take time today to correct a wrong that exists because of dishonesty.

The Do-Something  Girl

"Y OU LOOK like you're mad at the world," Amanda's mother said as she walked out onto the stoop and sat down beside her daughter.

"Well, I am," the girl snapped. "This street's a mess. Papers, cups, trash bags, overturned garbage cans—makes me angry."

Mrs. Stevenson nodded slowly. "It doesn't look very pretty, does it?"

"Nobody cares," the girl grumbled. "People just think it's a two-lane landfill."

Mrs. Stevenson studied the road thoughtfully. Amanda was right. Nobody cared about the feelings of the people who had to live beside the old lane. She'd lived on this street since she was a little girl.

Glancing over at her daughter, Mrs. Stevenson asked, "Well, Amanda, why don't *you* do something about it?"

"Me?" Amanda looked up in surprise. "I didn't make that mess."

Mrs. Stevenson shrugged. "It's not going to clean itself." She leaned down and whispered into the girl's ear, as if sharing a secret. "The world is full of complainers," Amanda's mom said. "What we need are a few do-something people who'll turn their anger into helpful action."

Mrs. Stevenson smiled. "You know, I've seen people whose lives were just like our street. They lived so carelessly. Everything to them was a mess, because they didn't care enough

13

14

about what they did."

The woman stroked her daughter's hair. "By choosing what's important to you and taking pride in everything that's a part of your life, you can help make your surroundings a better place to live. It's all up to you to be a do-something person."

"But I'm just one person," Amanda moaned. "And that's a big street."

She watched a tattered newspaper blow from a gutter and flutter against old Mrs. Montgomery's rose bush.

The kindly neighbor took pride in her flowers. Each morning Amanda would see her down on her knees digging out the weeds from the soil. The newspaper, the litter, the careless people, all robbed the white-haired neighbor's blooms of their beauty.

Amanda jumped to her feet and stormed into the apartment. Mrs. Stevenson called after her, "Tired of looking at the mess?"

"You've got that right," the girl

said over her shoulder. Quickly, she returned, clutching several large trash bags in her fists. "And I'm about to become a do-something girl right before your eyes."

Amanda lifted the bags high over her head. "Watch out, street. This means war!"

A passing dog froze in its tracks, unsure of what to make of the girl standing defiantly at the top of the stoop.

Amanda glared down at the statue-like canine. "And if you even *think* about overturning a garbage can, you'll have *me* to answer to."

The dog almost tripped over his own paws as he turned and fled.

Amanda worked all afternoon, collecting trash, sweeping the weathered sidewalk, and righting overturned garbage cans. By suppertime Amanda had transformed the whole street, and Mrs. Montgomery's rose bush looked lovely, bathed in the late-afternoon sun.

A tired Amanda was sitting on the stoop surveying her handiwork when her mother walked out of the apartment and gasped. "You've made our street pretty. I'm so proud of you."

The girl smiled a weary smile. "Yeah, but I was just thinking. In a few days it will be messy again. I can't make people be careful just because I cleaned up a little."

A car rounded the corner and sped along the lane. "Doesn't anybody else care?" Amanda asked.

The driver thrust his hand out the window. In it was an empty pop can. His fingers loosened their grip, then suddenly tightened again. Slowly he pulled the pop can back into the car. With a roar the visitor rushed past and was gone.

Amanda's mouth dropped open. "Did you see that?" she cried, jumping to her feet. *"He didn't trash my street!"*

Mrs. Stevenson nodded. "Looks like you made one person care. That's a good start!"

Amanda chuckled. "If I keep our road clean, maybe I can teach more people to think before they toss."

The woman placed her hand on her daughter's shoulder. "Jesus says the best way to teach others what's right is to *show* them."

Amanda smiled as the two headed for the kitchen. Many other jobs, all important to her, waited for the caring touch of the do-something girl.

BY CHARLES MILLS

15

KEY BOX

SECRET KEY:
Take pride in everything you do. Don't wait for someone else to do what you think needs to be done.

THINK ABOUT IT:
Do you keep your room, your house, your street, looking like Jesus lives there?

GO FOR IT:
Look for something you can do to make the world a better place. Ask a friend to help.

When Mother Called Tabitha

TABITHA, I would like you to go to the river and bring some water," Tabitha's mother said one morning. Tabitha lived out in the grassy country, in Tanzania, central Africa.

"Yes, Mother," sighed Tabitha as she picked up the waterpot and balanced it on her head.

Every day Tabitha went down to the river for water. On the shaded path, she would pass the little children who were playing with small stones. She would meet women coming up the path with waterpots on their heads. She would pass little boys on their way to school.

"Every day I have to go to the river—not just once, but sometimes two, three, or four times! It really is quite boring," Tabitha said to herself.

"When I finish bringing this waterpot up the hill, then Mother will say, 'Tabitha, I need more water.' Then I will have to go right back to the river again. I wish I never had to carry

another pot of water! I want to do just what I want!"

Tabitha walked down to the river, but she wasn't at all happy about it. She wasn't paying attention to where she was going. She looked around, and up at the sky. On her path she saw a beautiful tree with thick branches, dark leaves, and ripe fruit.

"Hey," said Tabitha, "this is my chance. I'll climb and eat all the fruit I want."

She set her pot down on the ground by the tree and climbed into its leafy branches. There she found a fine place to sit where the leaves were very thick.

"Nobody will see me here," she said to herself. "Not even my mother. I think I'll stay here all day long. I won't get hungry, because I can eat this good fruit. I won't get tired, because I can sit on this big limb. I won't get hot because the tree is cool. And I won't have to carry any more water today!"

Tabitha relaxed, smiling about her plan to escape Mother's chores. She sat up in the tree for a long, long time. She ate the fruit until she was full and could eat no more.

Back at home Mother worried. She said to her neighbors, "I wonder where my Tabitha is? Have you seen her?"

"No," said the neighbors. "We haven't seen her."

"She always comes back so quickly," Mother said, worried. "Tabitha has been gone too long. I should go and find her."

So down the path went Tabitha's mother. All along the way she called, "Tabitha, Tabitha. Where are you? Are you lost?"

17

From her hiding place Tabitha heard Mother calling. "I don't want her to know where I am," she said to herself. "I am not going to answer. I'll be very quiet. Then I will not have to carry any more water."

Quietly the girl climbed higher in the tree. "Now Mother really can't see me, even if she looks very carefully," Tabitha whispered.

The woman looked and called. But she could not find Tabitha. At last she started home. Tabitha could see her going up the path. "Now I can stay here, and Mother will never know," she said taking another bite of fruit.

Leaning back against a branch, Tabitha felt a sharp sting. "Oh!" Tabitha gasped in pain. "What was that?" she cried, tears welling in her eyes. Suddenly there was buzzing around her ears.

18

"Bees! They're stinging me!"

Tabitha hit one bee, but more bees came. And even more. Tabitha slid down the tree very quickly. All the way down, bees stung her head through her thick braids. They stung her eyes and her ears and her arms.

"Somebody help me!" she screamed.

But nobody answered. Nobody came because nobody knew she was

there. Tabitha ran all the way up the shaded path. Everybody had gone home.

"Mama! Come help me! Bees! Mama, do you hear me?"

Tabitha's mother ran outside. "Tabitha, where have you been?" Mother swatted and smacked the angry bees still buzzing around her daughter. "Here! Let me get those bees off you!"

The woman worked at pulling out the stingers while Tabitha cried. Her eyes and face swelled. Her ears and hands swelled. Oh, what a sight she was!

That evening when everything was quiet Tabitha told her mother where she had been and what had really happened.

"I am very sorry I did not come when you called, Mother," said the girl.

"I am sorry too," said her mother, "for a girl who does not obey is sure to have trouble."

"I have learned that very well," said Tabitha.

AS TOLD TO CAROLYN STUYVESANT BY TABITHA MOSES MWAMALUMBILI

19

KEY BOX

SECRET KEY:
Obedience and good sense keeps you safe, well, and happy.

THINK ABOUT IT:
Are there any times that you should not obey?

GO FOR IT:
Make a practice of doing exactly what your parents tell you. See if you notice a difference in how happy you both are at the end of the week!

A Stranger Helps Jesus

MAKE way! Make way for the King of the Jews," sneered the Roman soldiers. They pushed their Prisoner into the street. Pilate, the Roman governor, just released this Prisoner—a Man he thought was innocent of any crime—to an angry crowd. They wanted to see Him die.

Within minutes the news had spread all over the city. Everybody who heard about the case rushed into the streets. Soldiers were going to crucify, or nail to a cross, three men.

After placing heavy, splintery wood crosses on the backs of their prisoners, the soldiers ordered them to walk. Waving their whips, they shoved their prisoners down the crooked street toward Calvary Hill.

"Crucify Him!" someone called out. "Crucify Him! Crucify Him!" the people shouted. Soon a crowd had joined the procession, yelling and screaming, throwing rocks, and spitting at the prisoners.

Simon was passing through the city when he heard all the commotion. He was traveling from the African country of Cyrene with his family. "What is going on?" he said to himself. "Is someone in trouble?"

Simon rushed into the crowd to see, and his mouth dropped open in disbelief. What an awful scene. There on the ground knelt a Man too weak to move. People were cursing and kicking dirt on Him. The soldiers stood over Him, ordering, "Get up, get up! Pick up Your cross and get up that hill!"

It was Jesus of Nazareth. For the first time, Simon looked into the eyes of a Man he'd only heard about. His two sons, Alex and Rufus, had told him about this kind, wise, and gentle Man who healed people and performed miracles. Simon's sons also told him that they believed Jesus was the Son of God!

Jesus was trembling from exhaustion. Blood soaked His clothes, and the color had drained from His face. The people had taunted and jeered Him through the long night. Finally He had fainted under the weight of His cross. And no one offered to help Him!

When Simon looked at Jesus, compassion filled his heart. He wondered

how people could be so mean, especially to such a kind Man. "What can I do?" he said to himself. "How can I help Him?"

Seeing the sympathy in Simon's face, the soldiers grabbed him. "Here," they demanded, "you feel so sorry for Him—*you* carry His cross up the hill!" Simon's strong arms willingly lifted Jesus' cross.

The soldiers pulled Jesus roughly to His feet. Once again the procession moved slowly toward the hill. Simon followed, the heavy cross resting on his broad shoulders.

Turning, Jesus looked at Simon and saw the compassion in his eyes. The Saviour felt much better now, for He knew there was kindness and love in the midst of all that anger and hatred.

When they reached the hill, Simon watched helplessly as the soldiers threw Jesus down on the cross. He turned his head away as they pounded nails in His hands and feet. Simon listened in amazement. Jesus was praying that God would forgive everyone who had hurt Him. Simon saw the soldiers gambling for Jesus' clothes. He heard His mother, Mary, crying softly for her Son.

When Jesus said the words "It is finished" and bowed His head, Simon felt a great sadness, like something had died inside Him.

As Simon walked away, thinking about all he had seen, He was sure that this kind Man was the Son of God. From that day on, he would cheerfully do anything for Jesus.

BY BETTY DENNIS BROWN

23

KEY BOX

SECRET KEY:
Jesus always feels better when we show kindness to others.

THINK ABOUT IT:
Have there been times when you were mean and unkind, just because everybody else was?

GO FOR IT:
Search today for ways to practice kindness to people who need help. Make a list and talk about your ideas with your parents.

Pop Evans

THE SUN was hanging low when Bobby rounded the corner of Eighth and Vine on his way home from school. Pop Evans sat in his usual chair on the front porch of his cousin Vetta's house.

"Yo, Pop Evans, what're you doing?"

"Hey, boy!" Pop Evans raised his head and smiled. "Just sitting." The old man's gravelly voice sounded tired and thin.

"I'm feeling kind of poorly today, boy. Poor Vetta. I'm getting to be more and more of a burden."

"Hey, Pop Evans, you're no burden."

"Thanks, boy. I'm not complaining, but I know the score. I had a lot of good years."

"Yeah, and you're going to live a bunch more, too, I'll bet," said Bobby.

"Maybe so, boy, but I'm afraid they won't be good years. I've got Alzheimer's." He paused. "It's early, and my mind comes and goes, but the doc says it'll only get worse. It's in my family, you know. My great uncle lived to be 93, but the last 11 years he didn't know

his wife, kids, anybody. That's the direction I'm going."

"Pop, whatever happens, I'm going to look out for you."

"Thanks, boy. You're OK. Didn't mean to rain on your parade. It's just that I hate the thought of forgetting."

He brightened. "Say, boy, how's your basketball coming?"

"Pop, I'm getting good on the court. Now I can post up guys taller than me, and my turnaround jump shot is deadly. I've got me some bad head-and-shoulder fakes now, too." They talked a bit longer; then Bobby headed on home.

The next day the guys were hanging out after school.

"Look," Leon called out, pointing down the street. "It's that crazy old man from down the street." Leon Spencer Johnson was the resident bad dude at school. He made some decent grades, but he had one mean habit. He liked to make fun of people.

Pop Evans was shuffling down the street talking to himself. "Did Pop wander off again?" Bobby wondered.

"Yo, Pops, who you talking to?" Leon spat out. The guys all laughed and joined in the taunts, including Bobby. When the guys decided to rank on someone, if you didn't join in, they ranked on *you*. Still, it didn't feel right.

Just then a patrol car pulled up, and a police officer got out and gently took Pop Evans' arm. "Your niece is worried about you," she said quietly as she helped him into the car. The other officer glared at the now-silent boys; then they rode off.

"They should lock that old fool up," Leon said.

An uncomfortable silence hung in the air. Finally Leon said, "Yo, let's hit the courts." He stalked off slowly, followed by most of the guys. Bobby headed home. He circled to avoid passing Cousin Vetta's house. Maybe Pop Evans had seen him.

Bobby was quiet during worship and dinner. His parents knew something was really wrong when he asked to go right up to his room and study.

"Son?"

It was Dad.

"Yes, Dad, come in."

"Something's bothering you. Maybe you need to talk about it."

"Dad," Bobby started in, "did you know that Pop Evans wandered off this afternoon?"

Dad nodded. "I've heard."

"Well, he came over to our school, and, well, some of the guys were laughing at him."

Dad nodded again.

"I didn't help him, Dad; I laughed too. And now I feel like dirt."

Dad looked intently at his son. "Bobby, I know that was not the real you. Many times you've been about the only youngster around here to even notice Pop Evans. And I bet that you're about the only one with regrets over this." He paused, thinking.

"I never told you kids, but when your mom and I got married, I was out of work for about six months. I took some temporary jobs, but I could barely keep us housed and fed."

"Dad, you're making good money now, and we have all we really need."

"Thanks to the blessings of God—and Pop Evans." Bobby looked surprised. "That's right. Pop took me on

and helped me remap my life. He helped many people around here."

"Knowing that only makes me feel worse."

"Son, I'm not telling you this to make you feel bad. Soon Pop Evans is going to the rest home. He has gotten worse quickly. It's sad when a man does so much good and everyone forgets it. I'm telling you so when the right time comes, you'll let someone else know too. You and I will see to it that Pop Evans' good works are not forgotten."

It wasn't too many days after Bobby and Dad talked that Bobby found himself missing Pop. He stared at Pop Evans' favorite chair on the porch. Pop would be coming home for visits, but it was still lonely.

"Yo, man, that crazy old guy finally gone, huh?"

Bobby whirled around to find Leon standing there. "Look, man, let me set you straight about Pop Evans . . ."

BY BILL CLEVELAND

KEY BOX

SECRET KEY:
Love and respect for others changes a lot of bad into good.

THINK ABOUT IT:
Do you know a family member or neighbor who could use some care and attention? Who?

GO FOR IT:
Make and keep an appointment to sit and talk, bake cookies, or read with that person this week.

All Things Work Together

ON THIS sunnier than usual Friday morning Brianna and Taylor almost fell over each other running to the living room for worship.

Daddy smiled, "Who shot you two out of a cannon?"

"Tonight we're going to Grandma's!" Taylor answered.

"We're all very excited," Mother said with a smile. "Now, Brianna, please choose a song." After they sang a few songs Dad opened his Bible to Romans 8:28, and read:

" 'And we know that all things work together for good to them that love God, to them who are called according to his purpose.' "

"What does that mean?" Taylor asked.

"Well, son, it means that everything that happens to God's children will end up being for their best."

"Everything?" Brianna questioned.

"*Everything!*" Mom and Dad said in unison.

When they came home from school Brianna and Taylor ran into the house, up the stairs, and into their bedrooms. They collected a few items they had forgotten to pack for the long-awaited vacation.

"Sit down a minute, Bri," Mother said as she caught Taylor by the hand in the hall. "Children, Grandpa called. Grandma is sick, so they have to cancel the vacation. I know you both were looking forward to this, but these things happen."

The phrase "All things work together" ran through Brianna's mind again and again. "But Mom! Dad read from the Bible that all things work together for good. This isn't good! I don't want Grandma being sick. I don't want to cancel our trip. This isn't good; it isn't!"

"You're right, hon," Mother replied. "This isn't good. But the text means that all things, good and bad, will eventually work together so that God's children will praise Him for how it all turned out."

Taylor quickly wiped a tear from his cheek. "I really wanted to see Grandma Turner."

Before Mother could say another word Dad came in from work. As he entered the room the children knew that he already had heard. "I'm sure Grandma needs her rest so she can have us over another time," he said, putting his briefcase down. "But I bet you two forgot about the special program at the church tonight—that is, if anyone wants to go." Two faces brightened.

Before long the family was in the car and on their way to church. This Friday night was turning out all right, Brianna thought.

"Look at that hawk." Taylor said, pointing to a red-tail on a nearby fencepost.

"Beautiful. Look at those horses," Dad said. The family saw the horses. They saw a few sheep and lovely scenery all around. What they didn't see was a large tan truck running a stoplight. What they didn't see was it slamming them into a guardrail.

The sound of ambulances filled the air as they carried the Paige family to the nearby hospital.

The doctors released Taylor, Brianna, and Daddy with only minor cuts and bruises. Mother, however, was hurt very badly.

"Now, kids," Dr. Gordon said, "don't be afraid; we have everything under control." When he noticed Brianna's face, he stopped. "Brianna, you look very calm—not a bit afraid."

Looking directly into the doctor's eyes, Brianna said, "I'm not afraid, Dr. Gordon—I know God is working everything out. See, this morning my dad showed us in the Bible that all things, good and bad, will work out so that God's children will praise Him. I trust

30

2

Pass
Keys

William's Love Letter

THE HURRICANE had hit almost without warning, and trees fell into the small home that William lived in with his family. William held on to the tree branch with all his might. Trees were swaying, and pieces of wood and metal were flying through the air. All he could hear was the awful roar of the wind, and mothers screaming. Many people had already disappeared in the swirling, pounding waves. The flood was just about to sweep William away when just in time he got a tight grip on this large branch.

Everyone he loved had died. Everything he had was broken.

"Come, son, you're safe now," the rescuers said as they gently pulled William away from the tree. The storm had killed his mother and father and younger brother. No one could find any other relatives. William went to live in a shelter.

One month later a social worker put William on a bus. The bus took him to the next town to live in a strange house with a strange couple. Big tears slipped down the young boy's face and bubbled under his chin. He felt so alone.

When William finally arrived, the house and neighborhood surprised him. There was no paint on the house, and the steps were crooked. Where were all the trees? He couldn't make himself go in there. As he backed away, the door opened. He walked slowly up the steps and inside.

It was so clean in there! And right in the middle of the table was a big bowl piled high with apples, oranges, bananas, and cool bunches of grapes hanging over the sides. When he turned around he looked into the faces of a lady and a man. The lady had the kindest eyes. She came over and put her arms around him. "William, I am so glad you are here," she said.

William jerked away from her and said, "Don't you ever touch me. You are not my mother." Mr and Mrs. Brown had both lived a long time. They knew a lot. Mrs. Brown just picked up his suitcase and showed him to his bedroom.

For one whole year William didn't even try to be kind to either of them! The night before Christmas Mrs.

Brown sat down to talk to William.

"William," she said, "we love you so much that we really want you to be happy, so I'm going to send you to live with another family."

William didn't say anything, but his eyes got real big.

The next morning when Mrs. Brown went to the kitchen for breakfast, she saw a small box in the middle of the table. When she opened the box, there was a letter inside.

Dear Mama,

I've been too mean to you. It was me who spray-painted some of your roses with black paint last summer. I put chewing gum down in your winter gloves so you couldn't get your fingers in them. And if you are still looking for your scissors, I buried them in the backyard. But please don't send me away; just give me one more chance. If you decide to give me the chance, sit right next to me at the breakfast table.

Love,
William.

Mrs. Brown folded the letter and put it in her apron pocket. When William came down for breakfast, he remembered that it was a special day—Christmas. He could already smell the homemade wheat rolls and sweet-potato pie. But he really wasn't hungry.

William walked slowly down the steps and into the kitchen. Mrs. Brown was pouring the orange juice. Mr. Brown looked up over his glasses. They looked at one another, and all of them said "Good morning" at the same time. William pulled his chair out from the side of the table and sat down. Mrs. Brown put the small pitcher of orange juice in the center of the table. Then she walked over to the table, picked up her plate, and sat down right next to William. They just looked at each other and smiled.

Finally William spoke. "Mama, you and Papa are the best Christmas presents I have ever had." And Mrs. Brown said, "William, I am so glad that God sent you to share our home with us."

BY BERNICE WEBSTER

39

KEY BOX

SECRET KEY:
Family—whoever it is—loves, protects, and takes care of you.

THINK ABOUT IT:
When William wrote Mrs. Brown the letter, he called her Mama. Why?

GO FOR IT:
Secretly leave a special note for someone in your family, to tell them you love them.

Queen Esther's Day in Court

LONG ago in a land far away lived an orphan girl who became a beautiful queen. Hadassah was a little girl who lived in Medo-Persia long ago. When her parents died, she had no one to care for her. So her second cousin, Mordecai, adopted her. Mordecai was a worker in the king's courts and lived in Shushan, the capital of Medo-Persia. Perhaps dreaming of a day when she would become a great leader, Mordecai decided to give the girl a Persian name; he named her Esther, meaning "star."

Mordecai and Esther were Jewish people. Mordecai was proud of his heritage, so he carefully taught Esther the ways of their people. He also taught her to love the true God.

Now, it happened that in the same land King Xerxes was looking for a new queen. He decided to have a beauty contest to make his selection. His servants searched and found many ladies in the kingdom to be in this contest, including Esther. And Esther won! That is how she became queen of Medo-Persia!

Esther moved into the palace and

might have lived happily ever after had it not been for Haman. Haman was an evil and powerful counselor who worked for King Xerxes. He hated Mordecai. Haman hated Mordecai because he would not bow down to him when they met in the palace.

"You never bow down to Haman," said Mordecai's palace coworkers. "Why do you break the law every day?"

Mordecai never answered them.

Haman's hate worsened until he wanted to kill Mordecai. But Mordecai was one of the king's most trusted servants. Haman knew the king would be angry if anyone harmed him. Haman thought of an evil plan to get rid of Mordecai and all the Jewish people.

"Your Majesty," said Haman, "there are some people scattered around your kingdom who, unlike the rest of your loyal servants, refuse to follow your laws. There should be a law that they be destroyed!"

"Yes, they should be destroyed," agreed King Xerxes. "You see to it." He didn't know the new law would include his dear Esther, his servant Mordecai, and all the Jewish people. Haman couldn't wait for the day to come.

Something had to be done! Someone would have to speak to the king. But who would it be?

The news of the plot frightened the beautiful queen when she heard it. "I must go see the king," she said. Mordecai agreed. "Who knows? This could be the reason that you are in the palace as queen," he said.

Esther decided to go see the king and tell him what was going to happen. She would plead for the lives of her people. But this was very dangerous. The law stated that no one could see the king without an invitation. The penalty for entering the throne room uninvited was death! And although Esther was queen, she feared King Xerxes, for he could be cruel and unkind.

Three days before she went to see the king, Esther and all the Jewish people fasted. They asked for help from God. Then Esther was ready to speak for her people.

With determination Esther walked toward the throne room. Her gentle steps fell silent in the palace hallway. As she passed Mordecai she saw fear in his eyes.

"I am willing to die," she said. Mordecai nodded.

Esther opened the king's door. When it closed behind her, all became silent. Everyone in the throne room froze. The guards drew their swords, ready to remove this intruder. King Xerxes stiffened in anger.

Who dared to enter his throne room uninvited? He gasped. It was Esther. King Xerxes quickly extended his golden scepter, halting the guards. Esther bowed to the king and touched the tip of his scepter.

"Why have you come?" asked the king, relaxing a little. "Ask, and whatever it is, I'll gladly give it to you."

"Please, if you would, bring Haman with you tonight to a banquet I'm having."

Twice, Esther, the king, and Haman ate dinner together. Finally Esther exposed the evil plot.

"Your Majesty, may I make a request?" Esther said.

"Anything you wish," said the king, puzzled.

"Please, I ask you to spare my life and the lives of my people. Soon we will all be destroyed!"

"Who would want to hurt my queen or her people?" the king demanded. Esther leaned over and pointed to the wicked advisor. "Here is our enemy. It is Haman!"

Haman's face turned red. He fell to the floor and begged for his life. But the angry king ordered his guards to execute Haman for his terrible plot.

All the Jews were safe.

Esther never forgot her upbringing, her people, or her community. She did not allow her beauty or queenly status or the luxury and safety of the palace to keep her from living a loving, self-sacrificing life.

BY ELIZABETH WATSON

43

KEY BOX

SECRET KEY:
Remember your own family and community. It takes courage to stand for it at all costs.

THINK ABOUT IT:
It was good that Esther was queen when she was. Do you ever wonder why you are in a bad situation?

GO FOR IT:
Today do something to correct a wrong deed. Instead of ignoring a bully, talk to him or her about being kind.

Mitchell and His Reckless BB Gun

YOUNG Mitchell ran through the woods armed with his new BB gun, stalking through the bushes for easy targets.

Thwack! His first BB whizzed through the trees and landed quietly somewhere in a cushion of old leaves.

"I missed!" Mitchell whispered to himself.

Thwack! Thwack! . . . Thwack! He shot at trees and fallen branches. In the distance he heard the faint *plink* as one of his BBs hit a rock. On this quiet afternoon no one else was around, and Mitchell shot at everything he saw. Suddenly, he heard a soft rustle in the branches overhead. A clump of thick, green leaves wiggled about for a few seconds.

Thwack! Mitchell shot into the leaves and waited to see what would happen next. He strained to see a squirrel's tail hanging limply from the leaves. Blood dripped from the branch.

"Oh, no! I killed a squirrel!" Mitchell's heart sank. He stared up into the tree for a few minutes, then started home, ashamed that he had been so mean. Now one of God's animals was dead.

Mitchell Bush is a Native American and a member of the Onondaga tribe of the Iroquois Confederacy. His parents always taught him to respect life. Not only human life, but animals, fish, birds, and even plants!

He had never wanted to hurt anything. After shooting that poor squirrel, he made up his mind to be even more careful.

Mitchell really loved animals. As a child growing up on an Indian reservation in New York, when the dogs would try to find and kill baby rabbits, Mitchell would hide them. He cared for the baby rabbits by feeding them milk from an eyedropper. He felt happy because he was doing his part to protect them from danger.

When he grew up, Mitchell still cared for the animals and the trees. He taught people about the American Indians and how to take good care of nature. His family is from the Beaver Clan, so it's not surprising that beavers are his favorite animals. "Beavers can teach us a lot," Mitchell says.

"Beavers are hard workers," Mitchell explains to people who are curious. "They work and work and work. Beavers make dams and ponds, and this is very important. The ponds become homes for herons and geese and ducks and fish."

Farmers and hunters sometimes try to get rid of beavers. They shoot or trap the animals for their thick brown fur. Mitchell, however, works to see that they aren't all hunted down. Mitchell's family also helps the beaver by protecting its home—the beaver colony.

Other animals receive care and protection from Mitchell's neighbors and friends. They provide homes for animals and birds by allowing grass and bushes to grow, making a place for them to live. When harvesting plants, they make sure not to take all of a kind, but always leave some so more plants can grow.

An important lesson the American Indians teach about nature is that man is the worst enemy of clean air, clean water, animals, and pretty trees and bushes.

"Most people just don't care about nature," Mitchell said to a friend once. "It's a shame to see people throwing trash out their car windows."

Instead of thinking only about what we need and want, we must

think about others, Mitchell says. He was taught to think about his children, his grandchildren, and his great-grand-children when he has to cut down trees or throw out trash.

"We can all take the same care," Mitchell says. When we recycle trash

46

and protect animals, we're thinking about the children who will someday want thick woods to play in and green grass to roll on. They'll want beavers to watch, and squirrels that scamper about in trees.

BY PAT HUMPHREY

47

KEY BOX

SECRET KEY:
Be kind to the environment.

THINK ABOUT IT:
Are there ways you can be more careful around your house? What are they?

GO FOR IT:
Read a book this week on the environment. Then write down three ways you can help care for God's earth.

The Magazine

"MOM, can I go out and play basketball with the guys?"

"Have you done that job I gave you, Marcelo?"

"Yes, Mother, see?" Marcelo buffed one more spot on the table with his shirtsleeve.

Marcelo's mother smiled and looked at her son. Dancing beams of summer sun were shining in his eyes. She knew how much he loved basketball. And he was a good boy. "Sure," she said, "just don't be late for supper."

The boys were good friends. They had played together most days that summer. When the afternoon sun got really hot, they would go sit in the shade of the big oak tree and talk.

Rashid would talk about India, a faraway look on his face. Javier would make everyone envy him because he got to go to Puerto Rico. He spent part of his summer with his *abuelos* (grandparents in Spanish). "My grandpa would take me out on his boat every

day," he told his friends. "It was really fun."

Hung Ly would tell how much he missed his relatives who were still living in Vietnam. "One day I will make much money and go and bring them to this place," he would say.

Marcelo was a Christian and would sometimes tell them about Jesus and how he prayed to Him each night. Some of the boys could not understand—especially Rashid, a Hindu.

"What do you mean pray? To whom? And for what?" he would ask. Marcelo would try to explain to them that Jesus was his friend. The same way they spent time together, Jesus spent time with him. "I share with Jesus everything that happens to me," he would say.

Today a new boy named John joined the boys around the tree. "Hey, guys, you want to see something?" John asked.

"Sure. What?"

"Over here," he said, motioning toward the alley.

"Why do we have to go back there to see it?" Marcelo asked.

"This way nobody will bother us," said John. Looking around to see if anyone was near, John reached in his backpack and pulled out a magazine

49

that none of the boys had seen before. He was acting very strange.

"What kind of magazine is that?" asked Marcelo.

"Take a look. It has pictures of beautiful girls," John answered.

Marcelo had seen pictures of beautiful girls on the covers of magazines at the newsstand near the building where he lived. So he leaned over to have a look. Suddenly, his eyes grew real wide. "We aren't supposed to look at pictures like this! Where did you get this magazine?"

"It's my cousin's. What do you think?"

Marcelo felt uncomfortable. He knew that something was wrong. When John invited the boys to come closer and look at the centerfold of the magazine, Marcelo decided he had to get away from there. His heart was pounding in his chest, and he felt his face getting warm. He had never seen anything like this before. Marcelo turned to leave.

"Where are you going?" said John. "This too much for you? It won't hurt you! Come on, are you still a little kid or something? When are you going to grow up?"

John's cruel words echoed in Marcelo's head. It was all he could hear as he ran home. Marcelo walked straight through the kitchen, right past his mom, to the back porch. He sat, thinking.

"What's wrong, Marcelo?" his mother asked, looking through the screen door.

Marcelo began to tell his mother

50

what had happened that afternoon. She listened and then said. "I'm proud of you, son. You were very courageous to leave your friends behind and stand up for what you believed was right."

Later that evening Dad came and sat on the side of Marcelo's bed for a talk. "Son," Dad said, "I can see how that magazine made you feel uncomfortable. Pictures like that are not good because they are disrespectful to women. And looking at them makes people whom God made so beautiful seem cheap and worthless."

"Dad, I know you're right," Marcelo said. "God does not want us to look at women that way." "I never want to embarrass Jesus and you and Mom by anything I do."

BY SERGIO TORRES

51

Iris's  Business

"I WANT to own my own business when I grow up," 6-year-old Iris told her father. "I'll have lots of money and be my own boss."

Mr. Newman looked into the deep brown eyes of his daughter. He patted her curly head and said, "Well, child, what kind of business do you want to have?"

Iris smiled, eager to share her dream with this tall, handsome man who was her father. "I want to sew pretty clothes, expensive clothes, and sell them."

Iris lived with her parents in Kingston, Jamaica. She enjoyed their paradise home in the green mountains with soft breezes and colorful flowers. She lived a wonderful, carefree life, but already had big dreams.

Iris talked about owning a dress shop so much that everybody knew about her plan. Her parents encouraged her, praying that God would help her reach her goal.

After her mother taught her how to sew, the little girl began with pillowcases and tablecloths. Sewing a straight seam was hard at first, but she kept trying.

This is harder than I thought it would be, Iris thought to herself, but she kept at her task. She knew she must keep trying if she was going to succeed.

Iris learned to make aprons and curtains. Then she started making her own skirts and blouses. The more she made, the better she became.

53

One day when the pastor's wife came to visit, Iris's talent was discovered. "You are such an industrious child," Mrs. North exclaimed. "How would you like to sew for me?"

"Sure!" Iris responded quickly. "What do you want me to make?"

"I'll bring you some flowered material to make a large tablecloth with eight napkins to match," she said.

Iris got busy. She cut straight pieces of material and carefully hemmed each, making a beautiful table set.

When Iris was finished, the pastor's wife paid her well. What's more, she told her neighbors about Iris's sewing. Soon Iris was hemming and mending and altering garments. She wasn't making beautiful clothes and selling them yet, but she was getting the practice she needed so she could one day start her own business.

Iris's schedule was packed with activity. She busied herself every day with sewing, her schoolwork, and her home chores. She was so busy that she had little time to play with her friends. "Iris, you are always working," her friends chided. "Don't you ever want to have fun?"

"Sewing *is* fun," Iris told them. She actually enjoyed it. "And if I'm good at it, I can be a seamstress someday."

When Iris grew older, she opened her own shop. Her father helped renovate the shed behind the house. Iris hung up a sign that said "Open for Business."

Almost immediately Iris got a call. "Hello, I'm a friend of your pastor's wife. My daughter is getting married and we'd like you to make her wedding gown and all the bridesmaids' dresses." Iris was excited. Here was her chance.

She shopped for bright, frilly fabrics for the maids' dresses, and soft, satin material for the wedding dress. Then the sewing began. She used lace and hoops, brocade flowers, buttons and pearls. When she had finished, she knew she had created the prettiest wedding apparel around. How delighted the bride and all her maids would be to wear these pretty garments.

The pastor's wife's friend paid Iris what she asked for and even included a large bonus for her hard work. Now she had lots of money, and she was her own boss. Iris had realized her dream. She had worked hard. She had learned well. And she was pleased!

BY ELIZABETH WATSON

55

KEY BOX

SECRET KEY:
Good plans and preparation will help you realize your dreams.

THINK ABOUT IT:
Have you ever practiced and prepared for anything? How did you feel when you reached your goal?

GO FOR IT:
Practice this plan: 1. Make good plans. 2. Present your plans to God in prayer. 3. Set goals. 4. Work with all your might to reach them!

Moving  Day

LYDIA poked her mouth way out and wrinkled her forehead in a deep frown. She rocked from foot to foot, sighing with each step.

Her family was moving from her home in a small village outside Madras, India, to Michigan. Lydia's dad was going back to school. The whole family looked forward to it, except poor Lydia. She was angry and just didn't want to move.

Her mother prodded, "Come on now, Lydia, help with the packing. We'll enjoy living in Michigan; just you wait and see."

Reluctantly, Lydia started packing again. No amount of cajoling could lift her spirits. She simply did not want to leave India. She loved her village; it was her home. She loved visiting with the other girls at the community well where they drew their water daily. She felt comfortable wearing her long blouse and skirt. The constant warmth of the sun on her bare feet made her

feel good. The idea of living in ice and snow did not sound at all like fun to Lydia.

"Lydia," Mother called, "I need your help here in the kitchen."

"What do you want me to do?" Lydia asked halfheartedly.

"I want you to empty the kitchen drawers, and sort the flatware as you go," Mother instructed. "Then pack the silverware. Roll each glass in newspaper and put it in here." She gave Lydia a medium-sized box. "If you wrap carefully, the glasses will not break."

Lydia groaned as her mother continued. "Wrap each plate, cup, bowl, and saucer separately. Here's a large stack of newspapers."

"Is that all?" Lydia wailed.

"One more task," Mother said, ignoring Lydia's groans and sighs. "When you finish, empty the kitchen cabinets, covering or taping shut all the beans, rice, and flour containers so nothing will spill. Then pack them upright in that large barrel." Mother pointed to the proper containers.

Lydia looked at their kitchen. There was so much to do. The family had lived in this house all her nine years, and they had collected so much stuff!

Mother left the room. Lydia began

packing the silverware. Then she took down all the glasses and started wrapping them. "What's the point?" she muttered. "I don't want to move, and I hate packing. It's all going to the same place anyway."

She was getting angrier by the minute. *I could just throw all this junk into any box and be done with it,* she thought. And that, unfortunately, is just what she did. As fast as she could, she filled up all the boxes and sealed them with packing tape.

She surprised Mother by getting finished so quickly. "You're really a good worker when you decide to help," Mother said. "Do one more task, then you may go outside to play with your friends."

The next day the movers came, and

the family began their three-week journey to the States. By the time their travels ended, Lydia was really having a good time. Moving was not as bad as she thought it would be. When they arrived in Michigan, they busied themselves unpacking.

"Lydia, you packed the kitchen things. Would you please unpack them for me?" Mother asked. "Here are all the boxes marked 'kitchen.'" Mother smiled, pleased to find Lydia willing to help this time. "Organize the dishes and silver as you packed them; it should go quickly. After you're finished, you may go out and play with your new friends."

"OK," Lydia said brightly.

Lydia opened the first box. There were the beans and rice and flour, all mixed up in the boxes. Some of the dishes and glasses were broken. Oh, what a mess! Lydia had forgotten what a bad job she had done. She slowly began sorting the broken dishes and picking up the beans one by one.

Two hours later when Mother came to check on her, she was still sorting and unpacking, sobbing as she went. How ashamed she was that she had done such a poor job.

BY ELIZABETH WATSON   59

KEY BOX

SECRET KEY:
A job done well is complete the first time!

THINK ABOUT IT:
What would happen if these people did not do their jobs right the first time?
1. A cook. 2. A firefighter. 3. A plumber.

GO FOR IT:
You have a chore to do today. Whatever it is, do it once and do it right!

Uncool Calvin

H EY, MAN, look out!" Calvin looked up just in time to see a round orange object dropping out of the sky, straight toward him. It hit his head with a resounding *pong!*

"You all right, man?" A tall, skinny basketball player wearing a tattered T-shirt with a big number 25 printed on it knelt beside the 10-year-old.

"I think so," Calvin groaned.

"Sorry 'bout that, man. Guess my shot was kind of wild. Here, I'll help you up."

Calvin struggled to his feet and smiled weakly. "I'd better head on home now. I'm OK, really."

The boy in the T-shirt nodded, then hurried back to the basketball court at the far end of the parking lot.

Calvin rubbed his stinging forehead. He should've been frowning, but strangely, he felt happy. That basket-

ball player who'd just beaned him was none other than Jimmy Tomlinson, the most popular boy in the eighth grade.

That was the closest the mighty JT had ever come to even noticing Calvin. Maybe they'd become friends, shoot a few hoops together. All his friends would be impressed if he started running with JT.

The next day after school Calvin saw JT approaching.

"Hey, man," the tall boy asked, "how's the head?"

Calvin touched the dark splotch above his eye. "It's fine. Doesn't hurt." Calvin glanced around to see if anyone was witnessing this historic second meeting. "My dad said I'll have a bruise for a few days."

The two boys walked off in the direction of the bike racks. "Say," the tall boy said, "how'd you like to hang out this afternoon? I've got some sneakers I'd like to show you. What about it?"

Calvin couldn't believe his ears. First the most popular kid in school knocks him flat with a wayward basketball, and now this.

"Sure," the boy beamed. "Let's go!"

The two walked through JT's big suburban home and upstairs to his room. No one was home since JT's parents both worked. Calvin breathed a long, low "Wow" when he saw JT's TV, portable stereo—with CD player—and computer. All the latest Nintendo games sat stacked on the desk. JT showed Calvin his baseball card collection. Calvin had never seen such an assortment. JT even had an unbent Roberto Clemente in one of the boxes.

"Check this out," said JT, opening his closet. It was full of clothes. Expensive clothes. Leather jackets, cool suits. On the floor sneakers lined the wall.

"How can you afford all this?" Calvin asked. JT walked to his dresser. "Nothing to it," he shrugged. "I just

61

sell a few packs of this stuff, and I've got all the cash I need." He lifted a bunch of small plastic pill containers filled with what looked like yellow rocks. "Crack, man. It's like money in the bank."

Calvin gasped. "You sell it?"

"Yeah, on the corner, sometimes at school. No sweat. You just watch out for cops and wait for customers to drive by. My parents don't even know about it." JT turned. "Wanna try some? No charge."

Calvin jumped to his feet. "No way, man. Stuff like drugs, alcohol, and tobacco can kill you."

Jimmy laughed. "You sound like those stupid TV ads. I get high all the time. All my friends, too. You wanna be my friend, don't you?"

Calvin swallowed hard. For two years he'd dreamed of being "in." JT was everything he wanted to be—talented, athletic, popular. But drugs were another matter altogether. They're dangerous to the body. You can't get off them once you start. And they're illegal. The price for this friendship was too high.

"I gotta go," Calvin said softly.

"Suit yourself," the tall boy chuckled, pointing toward the door. "When you wanna get high, let me know. I can fix you right up."

Calvin shuffled his feet as he walked up the steps to his house. He

figured he had blown his big chance at being popular.

Several nights later the TV news reported yet another arrest in the neighborhood. The announcer revealed that police had arrested a teenage drug dealer on a street corner near the gas station.

As the police officers were leading their tall, skinny prisoner to the squad car, Calvin's breath caught in his throat. The frightened boy wore a tattered T-shirt with a big number 25 printed on it. JT wouldn't be selling drugs or playing parking lot basketball for a long, long time.

Suddenly, uncool Calvin knew he'd made the right decision. If being "in" meant destroying himself with drugs, alcohol, or tobacco, then he would just stay out. Even if no one noticed him, at least he'd be free. *That's* what's important.

BY CHARLES MILLS

KEY BOX

SECRET KEY:
Protecting your life from drugs, alcohol, and tobacco may not make you popular. But, it will give you your freedom.

THINK ABOUT IT:
Are you paying too high a price to be part of the crowd?

GO FOR IT:
Make a list of qualities that make a person important. Then compare yourself to your list.

Pass Keys Activity

person see you doing it. Just leave a simple message that says, "Love, your angel." When the person guesses it's you, choose someone else. See if you can break your own record.

For the Birds

It is our responsibility to take care of the earth that God has given us. One way we can do that is by taking care of His creatures. Try feeding the birds. Make this simple bird feeder by mixing any kind of birdseed with peanut butter. Either press it into a large pinecone and hang it using yarn or shape it into a ball and wrap yarn around it to hang it with.

Smiling Flowers

Cut off the top of a milk carton. Add some dirt, leaving about a half inch of space. Plant some flower seeds. Try marigolds. They are bright flowers and grow well.

When the flowers appear, plant them. Find a corner of your city, town, yard, or apartment that needs a little brightness. Or you can dress the box up by tying some bright paper around it with a ribbon and set it in a window.

64

Angels

Pick someone in your family for whom you can be an "angel." Your mission is to do something nice for the person you chose, such as: making his or her bed, straightening his or her room, or doing the dishes. But as an angel *you must not let the*

Fun Hunt

Print out this sentence: "A job done well is complete the first time." Cut out the words and put each one in a plastic sandwich bag.

Hide each bag. Using your Bible, make up clues about where each bag is hidden. For example: Turn left at the Psalm 92:15 (rock). Give your friends a map and invite them to try to find the bags. When they are done, see if they can unscramble the words.

In the Bag

Collect some useless items, such as a used envelope, a pencil stub, or the cardboard inside of a paper towel roll. Put one item at a time in a large bag.

Invite kids to reach in and just by feeling the item tell you what it is. When they have guessed, they have to suggest one thing that the item is still good for before they can take their hands out of the bag.

Enlist!

Join the war against drugs by starting your own "Drug Free" campaign. Begin by making up your own code. Use symbols on a typewriter or computer keyboard to stand for letters. For example: % = A, and so on. Or you may use numbers for letters like 1 = A, and so on.

Next write out messages about the harmful effects of drugs and alcohol and give them to your friends along with a copy of your code. Get some friends to help you start a KAD (Kids Against Drugs) Club.

3

Master
Keys

Wilma "The Mosquito"

WILMA'S eyes swelled up with tears again. The kids just wouldn't leave her alone.

"Wilma is a cripple!" they yelled. Once again their taunts pinched Wilma's feelings. She dropped her head as the tears trickled down her face.

It seemed Wilma was always sick. When she was younger she was often in bed with a dangerously high temperature, a sore throat, and sore muscles—she had double pneumonia and scarlet fever. Polio paralyzed one leg, and she had to wear a leg brace and walk with crutches.

And, because Wilma's friends cruelly teased or ignored her when it was time to play, she was always lonely. *Why,* she thought. *Why can't I be like everyone else?*

Many nights Wilma's mother and father would find her crying in bed. And many nights Wilma begged, "Dear God, please help me!"

"Don't give up, Wilma," Mother told her. "You keep working, and one day you'll get rid of that brace."

One morning Wilma woke up to find that her prayers had been answered, in a way that she had not expected. Her leg was still paralyzed, and yes, she was still sickly. But God had given her a new outlook on life!

"OK," Wilma whispered to herself, "I'm sick now, but I won't be sick forever! I will get better! When they tease me, I will not cry! And one day, when I am well, I will do something great!"

Wilma's new outlook was like medicine. She worked hard at getting better! She even faked not limping. Her mother and father found a new hospital for Wilma, and with proper

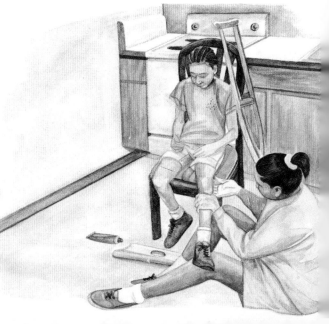

68

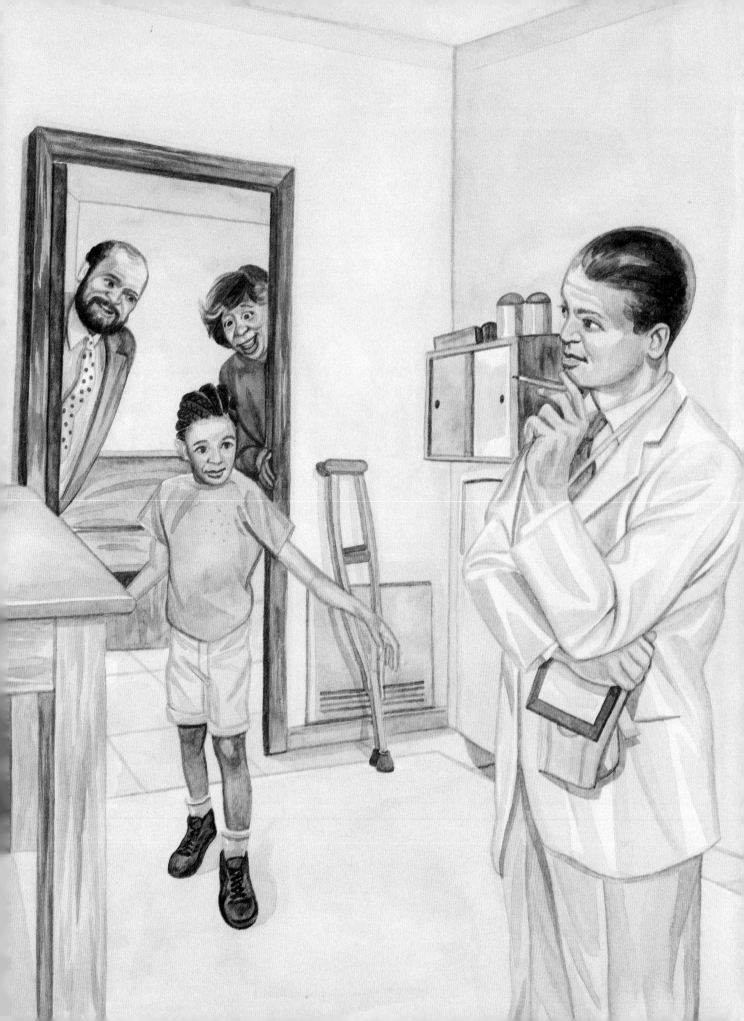

treatment she improved. Her brothers and sisters (she had 21) took turns helping her exercise and massaging her leg. And when Wilma's parents weren't home, she would take off the brace and try to walk.

Finally, something happened that made Wilma happier than she had ever been. Mother wrapped her leg brace and sent it back to the hospital!

"I'm well! I'm well!" Wilma shouted with joy. "At last I'm well!" Her determination had paid off.

Soon Wilma grew taller and healthier. She could run faster than other kids at school, and she could even keep up with her brothers at basketball. She practiced hard and played several sports.

By the time she was in high school, everyone called Wilma "Skeeter"—that's short for mosquito. She was so quick and fast—she buzzed up and down the court like a mosquito.

That little girl who could barely walk was running so fast at age 16 that she competed in the Olympics for the United States. And she did quite well—she came in third!

Then Wilma made a decision. "I will run in the next Olympics. And next time I will come in first!"

Wilma trained hard and practiced often. Finally she made it to the Olympics in Rome, Italy, in 1960. But tragedy struck again. The day before Wilma was to run, she fell

and twisted her ankle.

"Oh, no!" Wilma pleaded. "Please, God, don't let my ankle be broken!"

Again God answered Wilma's prayer. She hadn't broken her ankle. She would still be able to run! When she walked onto the field, the crowd cheered loudly. Wilma smiled and waved back. The audience was glad she had decided to keep competing, and their applause made her feel good.

"OK," Wilma said to herself, "I must not be distracted by the crowd. I must concentrate if I am to win." Concentrate is just what Wilma did. She entered three tough races and won the Gold Medal in all three.

Soon everyone knew Wilma Rudolph —the little girl who couldn't walk was now "The World's Fastest Woman!"

BY BETTY DENNIS BROWN

KEY BOX

SECRET KEY:
Determination often brings success. Keep trying.

THINK ABOUT IT:
What do you think about the way Wilma's friends treated her?

GO FOR IT:
In a small notebook, write down something you can't do now but will be able to do with some practice. Set a time or day when you will be able to do it. Work toward your goal until you can do it, and then write about it.

Billy Frank

"I JUST don't know what to do with that boy." The woman's voice sounded concerned. "Just yesterday he overturned our egg basket. Day before, he knocked my best china off the kitchen table. And last month that crazy kid sent our big chest of drawers crashing down a full flight of stairs. Scared 10 years off my life!"

"That's just awful," her friend gasped as their buggy bumped along the stony North Carolina road.

"But you know what happened this afternoon?"

"What?"

The woman smiled. "I was workin' at the sink, and in walks that boy of mine, a big smile spread across his tanned face, blue eyes just a-shinin'. He looks up at me and says, 'Here, Mom, these are for you.'

"Then he hands me a bunch of wildflowers he picked in the fields behind our house."

"Oh, that's sweet," said her friend.

"Sometimes he can be such an an-gel. Other times it's like the devil himself has control of my Billy Frank. He's not *bad*. He just needs an occasional reminder about how a proper Christian boy should act."

The buggy continued its bouncing journey toward the two-story farmhouse surrounded by red Carolina clay and oceans of summer corn.

Like all farmboys, Billy Frank rose at 4:30 each morning to milk the cows with his daddy. His boyhood was filled with hard work and simple pleasures.

One day a revival came to town. Billy Frank stood to his feet when the preacher asked if anyone wanted to give his or her heart to Jesus. Right there, under the sun-faded tent, with the soft crunch of sawdust under his feet, he made a decision. He wanted to obey the Lord from that moment on.

As the years flew by, Billy Frank's commitment to Jesus was tested again and again. He was smart and loved to read, but there was one interest he liked even more than books—girls.

He decided he would always treat them with respect. For example, he liked the movies, but his love for Jesus and respect for women kept him from going. "They show love and affection the wrong way," he told his friends.

Billy Frank also refused to go to dances. "Girls shouldn't be touched until after marriage," he insisted. "It's best to stay away from temptation."

The commitment to Jesus that Billy Frank had made in that canvas tent grew stronger and stronger. He decided he wanted to spend his whole life working for the Lord. *But how do I do that?* he wondered.

While attending a Christian college in Florida, a knock sounded at his door. "Come, Billy Frank," someone called, "I'm taking you to jail."

"To jail!" the young man gasped.

"Sure," the grinning visitor said. "Prisoners need to know about Jesus too."

Together they walked through the iron-barred doors of the dark and cheerless prison. They found a small group of men waiting for them in a little room.

The visitor, who turned out to be a preacher, said a few words, then told his listeners, "My friend Billy Frank would like to tell you about Jesus too."

Billy Frank blinked his eyes. He didn't know he was going to have to say anything. His knees began to shake, and his hands trembled a little, but he told the men about his decision to serve Jesus all his life. The more he spoke, the happier he got. *Hey, this isn't so bad,* he thought to himself. *I kinda like telling people about Jesus!*

And that's just what he did from then on.

His full name is Billy Frank Graham, and he's one of the most respected and dedicated Christian preachers in the world today.

Billy Graham, the farmboy from Carolina, has prayed with presidents and spoken before kings and queens. He's preached to millions of people in big open-air meetings in most countries around the world.

Maybe you'll be a preacher someday. Maybe not. Whatever you choose to do, make a commitment to your Saviour and give your whole life to Jesus.

BY CHARLES MILLS

KEY BOX

SECRET KEY:
Committing yourself to Jesus when you're young makes it possible for you to be a winner for God all your life.

THINK ABOUT IT:
Have you invited Jesus to come into your heart and show you how to be a loving, caring person?

GO FOR IT:
Ask your pastor to help you discover ways to tell others about the Saviour who loves them.

Ben's Best

GUESS what Carson got?" Ben's classmate yelled. The fifth-grade class had just finished a big test.

"I bet he got a big zero!" somebody shouted.

"Hey, dummy, think you'll get one right this time?" they teased.

"Carson got one right last time. You know how? He was trying to put down the wrong answer!" yelled another.

Ben tried to pretend he didn't' hear. But those mean words hurt him. Trying hard to hold back the tears, He just sat still. Even though his lips were smiling, on the inside he was crying. *I'll die before I let them know how much it hurts*, he decided.

"I guess maybe I'm just dumb," Ben mumbled to himself. He was beginning to really believe it, and so did everyone else.

For a while Ben continued to get poor grades. And the teasing didn't let up, either. Then one day, about halfway through the school year, Ben's teachers discovered that he needed glasses. Soon his math grades jumped from *F*'s to *D*'s. And for Ben, that was good. *Maybe I'm not so dumb after all,* he began to think.

But Mother wasn't about to let Ben off so easily. "You're too smart to settle for barely passing," she said. "You must get an education so you can be successful. If you keep on getting these kinds of grades, you'll spend your life on skid row or sweeping floors. You can do better. You're *going* to do better!" There was no doubt in Mother's mind. And she came up with a plan to prove it.

"Ben, you're not going out to play until you learn your times tables."

Oh, no, Ben thought. By the tone of her voice and the look on her face, he knew Mother meant business.

"And," she said, "you'll have to stop watching so much TV."

"But we don't watch that much TV now," Ben protested for himself and his brother, Curtis.

Mother didn't listen to a word Ben said. "From now on, you boys can watch no more than three programs a week." Now, that was really sad news. He would miss almost all his favorite shows.

Mother is really being unfair, he thought. But he didn't dare disobey.

Mother still wasn't finished. "And you're going to have to read two books every week. At the end of each week you'll report on what you've read."

That sounded impossible to Ben. He and Curtis complained all the way to the library. But Ben soon became fascinated with books. He read about

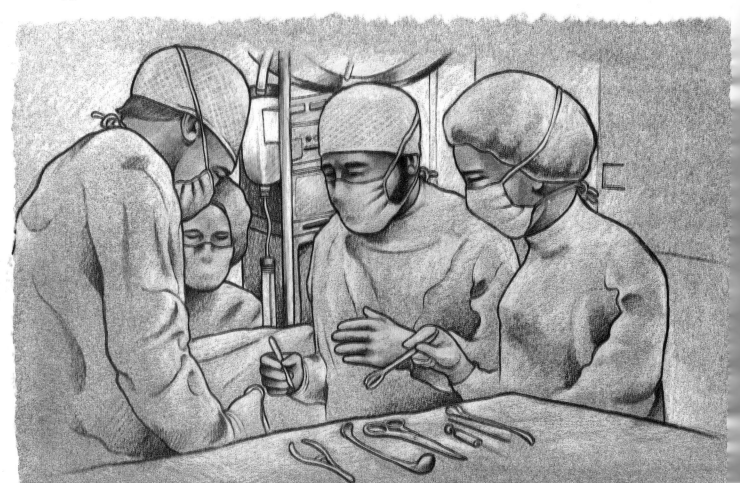

all kinds of interesting things—like beavers, squirrels, plants, and rocks. The librarian got to know Ben and Curtis well. She even had books waiting for them when they arrived.

Ben just kept reading and reading. Soon his grades began to surprise him, and everyone else, too. Without knowing it, Ben was learning.

In class one day Mr. Jaeck, Ben's teacher, held up a big, black, shiny rock. "Does anybody know what this is?" he asked. The room was quiet.

Ben wondered why nobody raised his or her hand. Then slowly his hand went up.

"Yes, Benjamin?" Mr. Jaeck said.

The room broke out in giggles. Surely Ben didn't know the answer.

"That's obsidian," he told the teacher.

"You're right," Mr. Jaeck answered with a slightly puzzled look.

Ben kept talking. By the time he had finished, the class knew everything there was to know about how obsidian rock is formed.

"Is *that* Bennie Carson?" somebody asked in surprise. His classmates couldn't believe their ears.

"I'm proud of you, Ben," Mr. Jaeck told the class.

From that moment on, Ben began to feel like a hero. Best of all, he started believing in himself. And on top of that, he was having fun learning. Now, instead of playing or watching TV, Ben spent his time reading books. It was as if he couldn't get enough of reading.

By the middle of sixth grade, Ben's classmates no longer teased him about being a dummy. Instead, they were asking him for help with their schoolwork. And it felt good to know the answers. He had become the top student in his class.

Ben's desire to learn and study kept growing. And so did his hard work and determination. When he grew up, Ben Carson became one of the best-known doctors in the world, all because he didn't let failure stop him.

BY PAT HUMPHREY

KEY BOX

SECRET KEY:
A slack, lazy hand makes one poor. Exercise for the mind builds power.

THINK ABOUT IT:
What about you needs improvement? Do you know how to improve?

GO FOR IT:
Become an expert about your favorite subject this week by reading about it.

The $500 Promise

YOUNG Eunice Geli did not know what to do. For months she had been trying to think of special ways to help her father. He traveled many miles each week, visiting churches in southern Puerto Rico that were under his care. Many of the people in those churches were very poor, and so the churches didn't have a piano or organ to play while they sang. Eunice's father carried his old guitar with him, but that was it.

Eunice would think to herself, *I want so much to do something to help Papi. But what?*

One day, as the family was window-shopping in town, 8-year-old Eunice spotted a beautiful and shiny black accordion in a storefront window display.

"I have never seen anything like it!" she exclaimed, her big brown eyes sparkling. She pressed her forehead to the window as she thought of a very good idea. "I want to learn to play the accordion so I can help *Papi* at church!" she declared.

"Thanks, *mijita* (my daughter)," said Eunice's father. "But the accordion costs $500. No one in this family has that amount of money."

Mr. Geli wasn't a rich man. The Gelis lived in a small apartment in one of the church buildings. Eunice and her brothers even had to share their family bathroom with the church members when it was time for church!

"Besides, Eunice, how are you going to carry that big thing?" Mother added. "It's almost as big as you are! How will you pay for it? Who will teach you to play it?"

Mother and Father quizzed Eunice about her request, but Eunice's mind was made up. She wanted that accordion.

"Papi," Eunice asked when the family returned home, "do you think the church can lend you the money to get the accordion we saw in town? If they do, I will pay you back in a year."

That was quite a promise coming from such a small girl. "I will pay back the whole amount," Eunice kept insisting. "You don't have to worry at all!"

After two years Mr. Geli had saved the two months' salary it took to buy

81

the accordion. When he finally brought it home, 10-year-old Eunice once again promised to pay the $500 back in a year.

Happily, Eunice took on the responsibility of paying for her instrument and learning to play it well. She could afford only a few music lessons, and had to learn mostly on her own. But soon she began to help her father at the churches. She carried her heavy accordion on her small back. Sometimes she would have to walk a long way to reach the church from the nearest road, but she never complained.

At the same time, Eunice earned money by selling magazines door-to-door. She sold to people in her neighborhood. She sometimes sold her magazines in front of the marketplaces, at the banks, the theaters, army bases—

anywhere where people were. Even though her magazines didn't cost very much, only 25 cents each, and it took a long time to save money, Eunice didn't give up.

"I must do what I said I would do," she reminded herself. With the pennies she earned from her magazine sales, Eunice saved enough in less than one year to pay back the entire $500.

"You are such a responsible young lady," her parents whispered in her ear as they hugged her tightly. "We are very proud of you!"

Eunice learned many things about responsibility that year. She discovered that being responsible may not always be easy, but it is always best. Being responsible helped her do the things she dreamed of. It also meant people could trust her to do a good job.

Responsibility helped her throughout her school years and even after she began working as a health consultant. So finally when the president of the United States asked Mrs. Eunice Geli Diaz to do two big jobs—be a member of both the National Commission on AIDS and the National Commission on Infant Mortality—he knew she would be responsible enough to do the job well.

BY RUEBEN ESCALANTE

83

KEY BOX

SECRET KEY:
Responsibility and dependability lead to respectability.

THOUGHT QUESTION:
What is responsibility? In what ways does responsibility make our world a better place?

GO FOR IT:
Can you think of ways you and your friends can show responsibility to others? to yourself?

The Triple Axel

ALL EYES were on Midori Ito, the 22-year-old, 4-foot-9-inch Japanese skater. The people in the stands waited to see her performance—Midori's famous triple axel jump was expected to win her the Olympic Gold Medal.

Midori was nervous. She skated shakily around the rink, practicing her jumps. As it got closer to the time for her to compete, it seemed it was becoming harder and harder for her to jump and land without falling.

Midori kept practicing. She smiled and greeted the excited fans waving their flags in the Japanese cheering section. Her strength and confidence made her a crowd favorite, and people liked her cheerful enthusiasm.

I must do well tonight, she thought. *They expect me to. I just can't let them down.*

Midori was a famous athlete in Japan, and her country had confidence in her. All of Japan looked for Midori to win.

Midori glided onto the ice, confident as ever. She gracefully swirled with the music. Gathering speed, she swept into one of her famous triple axels. She soared into the air, and then suddenly—oops!—she landed right on her bottom!

Midori bounced back up gracefully and continued her routine. It was almost as if she hadn't fallen. Three minutes into her program—her last chance to prove she could do it—Midori tried again. The large crowd watched breathlessly as she leaped into the air, spun around three and a half times, and landed, skating backward.

Midori beamed and the crowd cheered as the judges awarded her the Silver Medal for second place. She had become the first woman to perform a triple axel in the Olympics.

Midori's victory was a special one. It meant a lot to her and to many people who had been watching her for a long time. For one thing, success hadn't come easy. She practiced long, hard hours to become a world class skater. And like most of us, she had her share of trials and challenges.

Midori started skating at the age of 4. Most 4-year-olds think about playing more than anything. But not Midori. One day at the skating rink she saw a lady coaching some other kids. The lady's name was Machiko Yamada.

"Can I take lessons from you too?" Midori asked.

"Why, yes, of course you can." Machiko didn't usually take students that young. But when she saw Midori skate, she knew there was something different about her. She could tell that Midori was a little girl who knew what she wanted and how to get it.

Then when Midori was 5 years old her parents separated. It was a sad time for her, but she never talked much about what happened. Midori started spending more and more time

with her coach. Finally, at age 10 she moved in with the Yamadas. Midori was very happy with her new family.

School days were busy for Midori. At 6:00 a.m. it was off to the skating rink for practice until 7:30, time for school. Then at 5:00 p.m. she was back again for another three hours of skating practice.

When she was 14 Midori decided she would be the first woman to do a triple axel in competition. She entered the 1985 World Championships in Tokyo. That was a hard jump for the very best men and women skaters. Sadly, though, before the competition she broke her leg. It would be six months before she could start training again. Midori was disappointed, but she didn't let that stop her.

Finally, on November 2, 1988, Midori successfully performed the triple axel at a small competition in her hometown of Nagoya, Japan. But no one seemed to notice. The next week, however, at the All-Japan Figure Skating Championships in Osaka, Midori did it again. This time the whole world seemed to have been watching! And those who weren't soon heard about the young new skating champion. Midori had done something no woman had ever done before.

BY PATRICIA HUMPHREY

87

KEY BOX

SECRET KEY:
The cost of a win may include a few mistakes, a lot of hard work, and the courage to keep going.

THINK ABOUT IT:
Is there something you are afraid to do because the first time was hard ? Can you find someone to help you improve next time?

GO FOR IT:
The next time you make a mistake, don't give up. Think about what you can learn from your mistake.

Martin's  Fight

YOUNG Martin was so excited! He had just won first prize in a public-speaking contest. As he rode the bus back home to Atlanta with his teacher, he thought about how pleased the principal would be when he found out. Martin smiled to himself. Victory made him feel good inside, proud. But those good feelings soon evaporated.

"Get up!" ordered the bus driver. His tone broke into Martin's good mood. The driver scowled through the rearview mirror at Martin and his teacher.

They had just stopped in a small town, and new passengers were filling the bus. Many people were now standing in the aisles. Some frowned at Martin and his teacher. Because of segregation laws, Whites expected Blacks to stand and move to seats in the back of the bus. If there still weren't enough seats, Blacks had to stand.

But the Black people on the bus didn't want to move. Once again the bus driver looked over his shoulder and yelled, "Come on, get up! Get up out of those seats, or I'll have you arrested!"

Here and there, Black men and women stood. Martin stayed seated. He had never been so angry in his life. His thoughts raced. *I'm not getting out of this seat!*

The driver looked directly at him, pointing his finger. "Don't get uppity with me," he threatened, cursing and calling him names.

Mrs. Bradley, Martin's teacher, didn't want any trouble, though. "Martin," she said softly. "I know it's not fair; but I'm responsible for getting you home safely. Come on now."

Martin stood the whole 90 miles back to Atlanta. He hated segregation.

"One day," he promised himself, "I'll do something about this."

Martin kept his promise. Many years later the right opportunity came, and he attacked segregation head-on. In Montgomery, Alabama, where he pastored a church, police arrested a Black woman and put her in jail. She had refused to stand and let a White man have her seat on the bus.

When Dr. King heard about it, he exploded. "Oh, no, not this again!" he said angrily. "We must stop this abuse now! Tonight we will meet at my church. Please, tell everyone. Spread the word."

That evening when Dr. King arrived at the church, the crowd surprised him. The building overflowed with supporters. Thousands more who could not get in waited anxiously outside. Dr. King cleared his throat as he rose to speak. A hush came over the audience.

"Your coming here tonight lets me know that you are tired! Tired of being abused! Tired of being mistreated!"

"You're right!" the crowd roared as they cheered him on.

Dr. King motioned for silence. "We must refuse to take this abuse any longer. We must stop riding the buses! We cannot ride them as long as they remain segregated!"

The crowd cheered! "Let's do it!" they shouted.

The people found other ways of getting around. By Monday morning, when the bus boycott began, there weren't any Black passengers on the buses. Some people walked; others shared cars. Some people rode their bicycles. But no one rode the buses.

Many people in the city expected, however, that the boycott would end the first day it rained or got cold. Finding other ways to get around was hard. Many people didn't have their own cars. But Blacks didn't board a bus.

"We'll just stay off the buses until they get this whole thing settled," said one mother.

"I'm not walking for myself," said a tired grandmother, loaded down with packages. "I'm walking for my children and my grandchildren."

As expected, some in the White community decided they'd put a stop to the boycott. They called and threatened Dr. King almost every evening. His house was bombed, and also some of the city's Black churches. But Dr. King never gave up, nor did the people who wanted fairness.

Finally, after more than a year, the United States Supreme Court declared segregation on the buses illegal! Blacks could sit in any seat they chose, and they would be treated with courtesy! People all around the world learned from Dr. King the importance of fairness and equality for everyone.

BY BETTY DENNIS BROWN

KEY BOX

SECRET KEY:
Treat people, all people, equally.

THINK ABOUT IT:
What is equality? Do you know of any situations where people treat others unfairly and unequally?

GO FOR IT:
Can you and your friends help someone who has been treated unfairly?

Master Keys Activity

Popsicle Stick Puppets

Choose one of the stories from this section. Using index cards, draw each of the characters. Color the drawings and cut them out with scissors. Glue a popsicle stick on the back to make a hand puppet. Let the glue dry.

92

Now you're all ready to have a puppet show. Act out the story using your puppets. With practice, you can have a puppet show for the children's story at church.

You're My Hero

Look for the heroes in your community. Perhaps they are the trash collector who cleans up after your family, the police officer who takes good care of you, the teacher who explains difficult problems for you. Make your own hero/heroine award and give it to them.

Quality Concentration

On separate index cards, write the names of the people in each story and the character traits. These are the qualities they were known for, such as "determination," "responsibility," or "equality." Mix them up. Lay them facedown. Turn over one card. Now find the match in one try. If you're wrong, turn them back over. If you're right leave them faceup. Continue until all the cards have been turned over. To make this more challenging, make a card for each player in the group and his or her character traits.

Remembering Stones

It's important to make a commitment to certain things, such as doing your best in school, or not grumbling about your chores. Once you've made a commitment, try making a "remembering stone" to help remind you of your commitment. Find a medium-sized stone, preferably round and smooth. Paint it with pictures that represent your commitment. For school you might use pictures of pencils, books, etc. Put it somewhere you will see it often.

Who Am I?

On separate pieces of paper, write down the names of each of the people in this section. Place them face down and mix them up. Each person playing takes one paper and has someone else pin it to his or her back. Players ask yes or no questions about themselves and try to guess who they are. The game is played until all the players know who they are.

FOR SCHOOL-AGE CHILDREN
The Bible Story
This is the most accurate and complete set of children's Bible story books available. More than 400 Bible stories are included, with full color paintings at every page-opening. Unlike television, these stories introduce children to heroes you would be proud to have them imitate. These stories are also an excellent tool for loving parents who want their children to grow up making right decisions and making them with confidence. Ten volumes, hardcover.

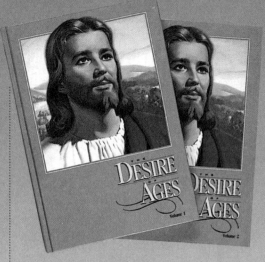

The Desire of Ages
This is E. G. White's monumental best-seller on the life of Christ. It is perhaps the most spiritually perceptive of the Saviour's biographies since the Gospel According to John. Here Jesus becomes more than a historic figure—He is the great divine-human personality set forth in a hostile world to make peace between God and man. Two volumes, hardcover.

Uncle Arthur's Bedtime Stories
For years this collection of stories has been the center of cozy reading experiences between parents and children. Arthur Maxwell tells the real-life adventures of young children—adventures that teach the importance of character traits like kindness and honesty. Discover how a hollow pie taught Robert not to be greedy and how an apple pie shared by Annie saved her life. Five volumes, hardcover.

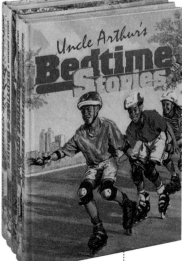

FOR PRESCHOOL CHILDREN
My Bible Friends
Imagine your child's delight as you read the charming story of Small Donkey, who carried tired Mary up the hill toward Bethlehem. Or of Zacchaeus the Cheater, who climbed a sycamore tree so he could see Jesus passing by. Each book has four attention-holding stories written in simple, crystal-clear language. And the colorful illustrations surpass in quality what you may have seen in any other children's Bible story book. Five volumes, hardcover. Also available in videos and audio cassettes.

For more information, write: The Bible Story, P.O. Box 1119, Hagerstown, MD 21741.

MORE *F*AMILY READING

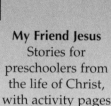

God's Answers to Your Questions
You ask the questions; it points you to Bible texts with the answers

He Taught Love
The true meaning hidden within the parables of Jesus

Jesus, Friend of Children
Favorite chapters from *The Bible Story*

Bible Heroes
A selection of the most exciting adventures from *The Bible Story*

The Storybook
Excerpts from Uncle Arthur's *Bedtime Stories*

My Friend Jesus
Stories for preschoolers from the life of Christ, with activity pages

Quick and Easy Cooking
Plans for complete, healthful meals

Fabulous Food for Family and Friends
Complete menus perfect for entertaining

Choices: Quick and Healthy Cooking
Healthy meal plans you can make in a hurry

More Choices for a Healthy, Low-Fat You
All-natural meals you can make in 30 minutes

Tasty Vegan Delights
Exceptional recipes without animal fats or dairy products

Fun With Kids in the Kitchen Cookbook
Let your kids help with these healthy recipes

Health Power
Choices you can make that will revolutionize your health

Secret Keys
Character-building stories for children

Winning
Gives teens good reasons to be drug-free

FOR MORE INFORMATION
on these books, mail the postpaid card or write:
Home Health Education Service,
P.O. Box 1119, Hagerstown, MD 21741.